For Diezel,
Wishing you the sweetest
of dreams!
Love,
Anne & Quinn

Dedicated to:
Jami Elaine Moutray.
We love you and you are
forever in our hearts.

Thank you, Tyler Arndt, for being a wonderful husband and amazing father. Because of you, this project that Quinn dreamt grew wings and flew. Special thanks to Alison Doyle, Jen Brekke, Melissa Boyle, and Marian Green. Your help, and most of all your support and friendship, made this project possible.

Most of all, I am grateful to God. Through You, all things are possible.

Fluff the Dream Owl

Anne Moutray Arndt & Quinn Arndt
Illustrated by Lauera VanderHeart
Edited by Marian Green

Published by  Inspired Minds, LLC
Copyright © 2014 by Anne Moutray Arndt

All rights reserved. No part of this publication may be reproduced, distributed, or transmitted in any form or by any means, including photocopying, recording, or other electronic or mechanical methods, without the prior written permission of the authors, except in the case of brief quotations embodied in critical reviews and certain other noncommercial uses permitted by copyright law.

"Mommmmmmm!"

Quinn cried out, waking himself from *another* scary dream.

He ran to his mom's room and leapt onto her side of the bed.

"What's going on, Quinn?" His mom asked, as she wrapped him in a bear hug.

"Those mangy, mop-eared monsters were chasing me again!" Quinn cried.

"Nothing in your dreams can hurt you, honey. Dreams are just your mind telling stories," she said.

"Yeah, maybe," Quinn said. But he still felt afraid.

Mom got out of bed. "I remember when monsters were real to me, too. I know just what we can do about this," she said.

She walked over to her closet, opened the door, and pulled out a sparkly treasure box.

With the treasure box in hand, Quinn's Mom took Quinn back to his room. She tucked him into his own covers before opening the box. Inside was a fluffy, stuffed owl. The owl glowed white in the dark night of the room. "I had bad dreams, too," his Mom said, with a twinkle in her eye, "until my mom gave me this."

"He is yours now. Name him what you wish. When you fall asleep with him, you'll feel safe. You will see," she said. Then she kissed him goodnight.

"I'll call you 'Fluff,'" Quinn said. And with his new friend tucked beside him, he closed his eyes and drifted off to sleep.

Once again, the dreams came. Once again, they were filled with mangy, mop-eared monsters. But just as Quinn felt afraid, Fluff appeared!

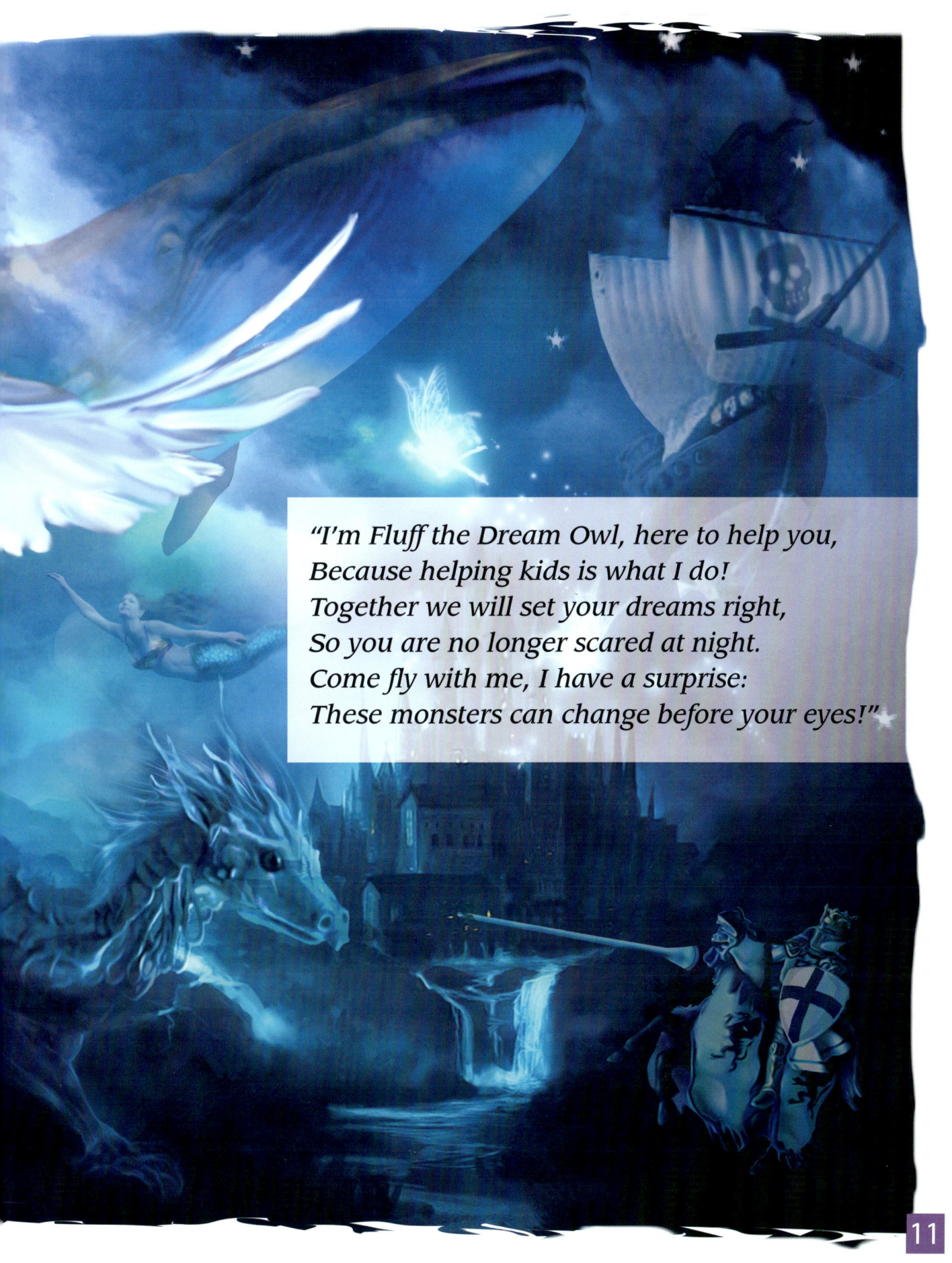

"I'm Fluff the Dream Owl, here to help you,
Because helping kids is what I do!
Together we will set your dreams right,
So you are no longer scared at night.
Come fly with me, I have a surprise:
These monsters can change before your eyes!"

"Imagination is your mind at its best,
But those scary thoughts can steal your rest.
When creatures show their monster teeth—sharp, white, and scary,
Turn those creatures into gumdrops—lemon, lime, and cherry!"

Fluff took a deep breath and closed his eyes.
"Ya-hoooo! Ya-hoooo!
Look what we can do!"

Quinn looked on in amazement as he saw the gumdrops, one in every color. "**Wow!** Those monsters look delicious!" he exclaimed.

"Ya-hoooo! It's true!
Look what we can do!
I imagine fun thoughts in my mind,
Until the scary is far behind.
Now show me the magic in your head—
You don't have to be afraid in bed."

Quinn thought of something fun, took a breath, and closed his eyes. He let out a **"Ya-hoooo!"**

Quinn opened one eye and looked at Fluff, "Am I doing it right? I don't see anything."

Fluff wrapped a wing around Quinn's shoulder.
*"It takes lots of practice—and patience, too.
Stick with it and you'll see what you can do.*

*Take a deep breath, then think of the best.
Your imagination will do the rest."*

Quinn thought of something fun, took a breath, and closed his eyes. "Okay I'll try again," he said as he let out a **"Ya-hoooo!"**

WOW!

Fluff gave Quinn a high-five!
"Way to go Quinn, you did it.
You kept trying and didn't quit!
You can, indeed, change the stories in your dreams,
And make them into fun and silly things!"

Quinn considered Fluff's words. "A-ha!" Quinn exclaimed. "It really is my imagination that creates the scary monsters. I don't need to be scared because I can change the stories in my head.
It's my mind; imagination is key—
It unlocks scary dreams and sets me free."

"Keep good thoughts in your mind before closing your eyes each night,
This will make it easy to keep your dreams happy and bright!
If those scary creatures do creep into your head,
Remember, you can make them friendly instead!"

From that night forward, Quinn slept with one arm wrapped around Fluff until...